what is miranda looking at?

3 2901 00422 4573

© Hardenville s.a.
Andes 1365, Esc. 310
Edificio Torre de la Independencia
Montevideo, Uruguay

ISBN 9974-7896-1-3

Printed in China

what is miranda looking at?

Texts

Mariana Jäntti

Illustrations

Mariana Jäntti

Design

www.janttiortiz.com

Miranda watches life unfold before her eyes.

Miranda looks
through the window,
a rainy day...
a quiet street...
an emptiness.
Suddenly, it changes!

A huge red umbrella
passes by...
Who is that woman
in the flowered dress
and fancy shoes?
Where is she going?
Who is she looking for?

After so much rain,
the sun comes out.
Miranda goes
with her mother
to her aunt's house
not too far away.

While the adults talk,
Miranda sits alone,
watching the people go by.
All of them look
unfriendly and grim…
what's wrong with them,
anyway?

Then, Miranda
imagines them differently
– transformed by a fairy
from grumpy and grim
to happy and fun.

Afterwards,
Miranda and her mother
take the subway home.
There are people
everywhere...

On the train,
Miranda hears music.
A man is strumming
his guitar
and singing a song.
It's a party!

The train pulls up to Miranda's stop,
"We're home," sighs her mother,
looking very tired.
"Were you bored, today?,"
 she asks wearily.

A little confused,
Miranda looks back
at her mother
"Bored?," she says
"Oh, not at all!
It was so much fun for me!"

And puzzled,
Miranda wonders,
"Where was SHE?"

WHAT IS MIRANDA LOOKING AT?

This story is about Miranda's discovery of life's many gifts. Gifts often remind us of our childhood, and even though we know that life's gifts are not always a result of our actions, we often believe that we deserve them. We fail to value these gifts, and often are not grateful for them.

Like most children, Miranda is aware of life's gifts every step of the way. She is trusting, she does not judge, she has no expectations of the world. She feels all the small moments of life in her heart, and she is thankful for them. She enriches them with love, fantasy, imagination and creativity, transforming them into moments of magic, living each instant as a unique gift.

What Is Miranda Looking at? reminds children never to lose sight of the gifts of life, which as adults we often miss in the bustle of our daily lives. The story also warns us not to take life's gifts for granted.

MARIANA JÄNTTI

WISHING THAT THE CHILD NEXT TO YOU
HAS ENJOYED THE STORY AND SHARED A MOMENT OF LOVE

nicanitas
BOOKS FOR CHILDREN

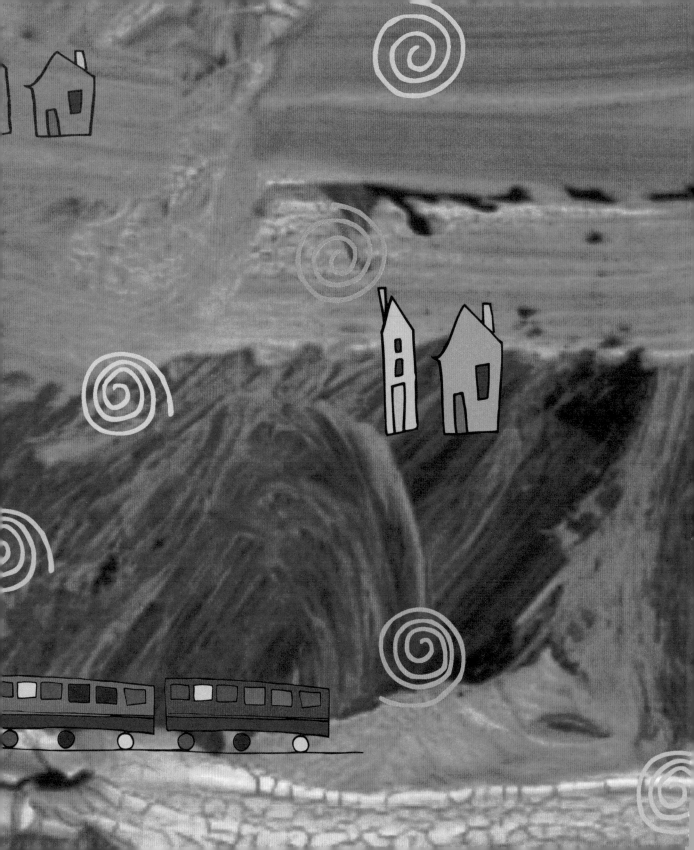